On A Bender Abroad

MIKE LEMCKE

This book is a work of fiction. Names, characters, places and incidents are either products of the authors imagination or are used fictitiously. Any resemblance to any events or locals or persons, living or dead, is entirely coincidental.

To my parents,
who have always supported me
in my comedic endeavors.

MIKE LEMCKE

Table of Contents

MIKE LEMCKE

La Vita é Birra
(Life is Beer)

At 5 a.m. I pulled on some clothes and hit the street. The nightclub neon signs were just dimming as the sun broke over the Alps. It had been a restless night as the vibrations from the city rang in my ear, car horns and distant shouts calling out in the night. Twenty hours prior I had arrived, but I still didn't feel like I had touched down. The Italy that I had been daydreaming about was just out that hotel window, two flights down and ready to be enjoyed. I have never been very good about bottling my emotions when I first reach my destination. It was a New Year and I couldn't wait to pop the champagne.

The empty streets slowly came to life as the background extras took their places. Shopkeepers began rolling up their metal doors, old ladies swept the sidewalks in front of their stores and portly deliverymen leaned against their trucks having their morning cigarette. I was happily and thoroughly lost by the time the coffee shops opened and the day players emerged. Businessmen in dapper suits stood drinking espresso at the bar, slender beauties walked by with purse-sized dogs and Italian stunt drivers barreled down narrow streets in their miniature vehicles, screeching around corners and jolting through intersections before bouncing their way into undersized parking spots.

At some point you have to try out using the language, so I decided to pop into a café and give it a go. On my short walk to the front I came up with a well-crafted and silently rehearsed sentence. It was filled with charm, doused in wit and all throughout graciously polite, but when the words came out they were less of the poem-like stanza I had composed and more of a stuttering incoherent noise. By the time my tongue kicked it around and my lips groped the vestiges, it sounded like a trumpet player falling down a staircase. The second attempt was muffled and inaudibly delivered, like an unskilled spy speaking in code. The barista's only response was a slow rise of her eyebrows. Cheeks hot and in a panicked sweat, I cut out all the fancy bits to a shortened and sheepish 'Un cappuccino, per favore.' If I hadn't just ordered something I would have run out of there. This is just how it is with language sometimes; you're either a high wire act or a falling clown, a fire juggler or an arsonist, a lion tamer or a guy with a stool and a whip who's just shit his pants.

I still hated to be that guy though. Americans are constantly labeled as uncultured. This mainly stems from our lack of knowledge when it comes to language and geography. Europeans give us grief, as if they aren't a 2-hour train ride from a being in a different country, tasting exotic food and listening to a foreign language. Growing up in the U.S. we just have Canada, which is a lot like America, just colder and the people are nicer. Then we have Mexico, but let's be honest here, Mexico is shady. I mean you can't even drink the tap water there. You drink tequila for two weeks straight because it's the water that will fuck you up.

"What happened to Mike? Why is he passed out on the ground? Did he drink too much tequila?"

"No, he was brushing his teeth and he rinsed."

The toughest part about being an American abroad is all of the associations that come with it. Usually I try to avoid the situation entirely by telling everyone that I am from California. It comes with a different connotation. Instead of talking politics or foreign policy we would talk about movies and surfing.

Pardon the cliché, but after being abroad you realize that people are people; they just come from different cultures and different walks of life.

I have met a lot of people who have traveled to America, and the conversation always seems to go along the same lines.

"While I was in the U.S. the people were really nice, very hospitable and friendly. I don't know… to be honest before going I thought they were all going to be arrogant jerks."

This whole concept has always struck me as odd. I would never go to a country filled with bastards; it's just not how I pick my travel destinations. I don't know how one would explain it to others.

This summer you just have to join me. I'm going to this country that is just riddled with assholes. It's fantastic. It's just absolutely littered with douche bags.

Here is a picture of us from last year at the general

attraction; you have to strain a bit to see it, as people were intentionally walking in front of the camera and the old lady in the background kept holding up both her middle fingers. The whole country is like this. It's truly something special.

Oh and here, this one is great. I left my phone at a restaurant table and the waiter took this picture. That's not an entrée, that's an undercarriage.

On the walk back I felt a palpable energy like on many morning walks to come, I was filled with emotions of equal parts exhilaration and shame. When I arrived at the hotel just about everyone in the study abroad program had made their way to the breakfast table, save for my brother Charlie and my good friend Franklin, who were either nursing a hangover or a morning beer.

I guess you could say my older brother and I are close, if by close you mean two guys that lived in the same room for 16 years, hung out on weekends, went to the same college, shared all their secrets, shared all their jokes, and made a promise to each other to spend a year abroad, and were living it out at that moment, close. If we were any closer to each other we would probably speak exclusively in our own twin language.

My brother had met Franklin in an Italian class his freshman year and he quickly became family from that time on. He had many of the same tastes, the same humor, the same passion for Italian language, and the same love of the adventure that Europe offered. He loved a good story, he told a good story and he quickly became part of our shared folklore.

The large dining room was filled with unfamiliar students from all across the States. There was strange forced social interaction and I don't know how to best describe it, but the energy was somewhere between speed dating and an Alcoholics Anonymous meeting. Not having been laid in awhile and in desperate need of a drink, I sat down at a table of characters I would be imbedded with for the next ten months.

In Stephanie's eyes you could see both an angelic purity and a glimmer of mischief. She had an almost Amish quality about her. Maybe she didn't speak Pennsylvania Dutch. Maybe she didn't have a religious objection to the use of electricity. And maybe she didn't come from a long proud line of people that loved facial hair yet hated mustaches, but she was definitely on a Rumspringa of sorts. I would later meet many others like her who had bailed on the barn raising to embark on a year of freedom, to participate in an institutionalized rite of passage, partaking in almost pre-calculated misbehavior: living among the English, drinking, experimenting with drugs and engaging in sex, before returning to the farm and taking the big plunge into the world of identical dress, one room school houses and living up to the expectations of their elders.

If Rob's mohawk wasn't a dead give away, you could tell by each anecdote he told that he was a party animal. He was the kind of guy that would turn any weekday into a night out and any weekend into a bender. To be honest I think he was just an excitable boy.

You have to be careful around people like this. Any ordinary task is escalated into a festivity. *Breakfast? I have the champagne. In between classes? There's a pub down the street. Going to the museum? Let's do mushrooms.* The only thing I held against him was that Rob insisted that he be called Roberto as if his legal name had taken in-flight Italian on the way over.

Katy, bookish looking girl, sat next to me in silence, with her prop-like bowler hat and a plate of partially nibbled fruit. She was either from a different time or in a different world. We had a couple of brief exchanges, but I was pretty sure she was really just thinking about what was going to happen next to the headstrong female character in the book poking out of her bag.

Sara was a long distance runner. She spent the better part of 10 minutes talking about her boyfriend, Jake, an ocean away. It didn't take a rocket scientist-psychiatry double major to tell that she was trying to fool herself into thinking that she wasn't fleeing an all-too-serious relationship and trading one finish line for another. 20 is not a good age to have your lover be in a far away land. I kept wondering when Jake was going to figure out that sending his blue-eyed, lightly freckled brunette off to a country known for its romance, wine and notoriously bold, well dressed men, whose only mode of communication is a wildly seductive language, might have been a bad call. I tried my best to sound upbeat, but my - "Well, I hope it all works out," fell flat. I'm not going to lie, it was a belly flop. I attempted a recovery with an "Oh, you'll be fine," which accidentally was accompanied by a compulsory slight head turn; the same involuntary reflex a medic in an army movie has when he suddenly notices a shockingly unfixable belly wound.

We used different guises. We claimed to be learning culture and studying language and becoming citizens of the world, but behind the curtain we were just dreamers, drinkers and hopeless romantics.

After introductions were out of the way the table talk became drab. The others had transitioned the conversation into small talk about their trip in quintessential tourist fashion. You've heard it before. They complained about travel; single servings, the chicken on the plane, the length of the connection on the cheap-ass flight they themselves had purchased. Who am I to judge? I guess people travel for different reasons. Some people travel to take stock photos, dig through fanny-packs for portable conveniences and do their best not to veer off the well trod path. They don't care for the journey.

I, like some, enjoy the experience of the experience. The little inconveniences of travel are all part of the buildup. I relish them. The dry chicken is a precursor to the fresh *mozzarella di bufala*, the watered down coffee is a foreshadow of the rich espresso and hopefully the morbidly obese person sitting next to me in 22F has a smoking-hot-bizarro-doppelganger waiting for me in the hotel lobby where I land.

I mean give me a break. Do you think Lewis and Clark argued over who got the aisle seat? You think that astronauts complained about the taste of tang? Or deep-sea explorers bitched about the legroom? We just crossed an ocean; it used to take scurvy to get here.

And what's an adventure without getting lost, finding a hidden place and engaging in the occasional awkward exchange? If you want the same experience as everyone else; save yourself the cash, superimpose yourself on a post card, drink a box of wine and watch Rick Steves take your vacation. For me, you could leave all the guidebooks in alphabetical order at the library. I don't really see the rationale in planning out your quest so that it reads like a choose-your-own-adventure novel.

Don't get me wrong; when I travel I do make a point of seeing some of the main attractions. If I'm in Paris, sure, I'll go to Notre-Dame, I'll ride to the top of the Eiffel Tower and I'll check-off some pieces at the Louvre. But the main exhibition is never the highlight, and never really the focal point for me. I prefer being in the next room watching a heavy set Eastern European man argue with a museum docent as to whether or not he touched a painting; as opposed to standing in a line of smelly damp tourists; nudging, elbowing, and falling over each other to see an 8½ by 11 painting behind 3-inch glass of an unattractive chick with a facial expression that so clearly demonstrates just how bored she is with the whole situation. And sure it's unique for a painting, but believe it or not I have had a lot of homely girls follow me with their eyes as I left the room unimpressed and wondering to myself why I had made the effort in the first place. Meanwhile, if you can peel yourself away, the guy reeking of potato pancakes just made a reference to somebody's mother and the docent looks like he is about to turn his maglite into a blunt object.

After shifting in my seat about twenty times I stood up and left the table. Charlie, Franklin and I, found ourselves at the coffee cart out of the same boredom and the need to get away. The conversation was brief and filled with the same propelling thoughts.

"I gotta get out of here."

"I need a beer."

"I saw a café down the street."

"They have beer?"

"And a couple of cute waitresses."

"Sounds like a plan!"

Collectively we turned in one motion toward the door. Behind us the sound of clanking silverware and dull tourist banter crossfaded into the sharp reverberating city in motion; sounds of revving engines and morning greetings, sounds of people with somewhere to go, and sounds of people who have just arrived, and in the mix of it all, the vibrant sound of life getting started in the Italian city.

Mustard's Last Stand

The night began calmly enough with a game of *Risiko*, the Italian equivalent of the board game Risk. A small group of international students had accumulated at our apartment in preparation for a night on the town. The rain had picked up and we made the collective decision to kill off a couple hours till it died down. Our friend Geraldo ran across the apartment complex to grab his game of Risk, bringing back with it his roommate Kevin, who we called by his last name; a more entertaining Mustard. His title worked well, as he was somewhat of a condiment to the group. We only brought him out on certain occasions, he went with about everything and you could usually find him on the side.

Mustard kept to himself most nights. He had a certain reservation about him, common of a guy who stayed home and attended city college before passing on to a four-year school. By the time he mixes in with those that have been living the college lifestyle; his clothes, haircut and age are a little outdated.

The Game

Risk is a fascinating game of strategy in which a player attempts to conquer the world. It's a board game where the board itself is a map of the world. It's not an accurate map like one you would find in an atlas, but yet looks as though I, or perhaps a ten-year-old child had attempted to draw it. The continents are clumsily sketched, the borders are vague, and the countries listed may or may not exist in real life.

"Is Ural a country? It used to be? Well, I'm leaving it."

How to Play

After the players have used their plastic pieces to claim each country, people begin to attack each other. The attacking and defending players role their dice, with the lower number losing their respective pieces.

The objective of Risk is to occupy every territory on the board, eliminating all other players and maybe a friendship or two, thus conquering the world. A complete game takes 3 hours and may, in all likelihood, result in adverted eye contact and minimal conversation between you and your roommate for the next two months.

In Risk it is common for one person in the group to get way too into the game and under a thinly veiled guise of 'play' emerges the dark inner workings of human nature. As the player gets more out of control, the other players stand watch and learn the true answer to whether or not the world could ever live in peace.

"Take that fucker! All you bitches are going down." Mustard declared after he rolled sixes. "Now I'll take you in Mongolia."

Mustard was in full form. He was acting like his rolls were a representation of his sheer talent and intelligence, as opposed to just blind dumb luck. The man was Napoleon reincarnate. Mustard pointed his sharp slender nose.

"Give me a card fucker! I gotta piss."

In his absence we quickly formed an alliance to topple the great dick-tator. Suddenly the game turned. The dice stopped cooperating with their bloodthirsty commander. Mustard began yelling at them as if they were a lover he had caught cheating. "Snake eyes? Fucking skank!"

When we finished eliminating him from the game we celebrated by ending the game right then and there. His roommate poured shots for the group and we toasted with smiles resembling those of the Allies parading down the Champs Elysees. We folded up the game and ramped up the music and the drinking.

Mustard began dangerously pouring himself shots from his bottle of Jaeger and unleashed on a rant. "You're such a dick man. This is bullshit, you guys can't just stop the game. There aren't teams in this game, it is about taking over the world..."

Franklin, in an attempt to ease the tension that was building, went over to the piano in the corner of the room and with a cigarette hanging from his lip, began playing a melody that was at first unmistakably familiar, then quite obviously *Imagine* by John Lennon.

Imagine there's no countries, It's not hard to do,
Nothing to kill or die for and no plastic armies too,
Imagine all the people living for to-nigh–high-ight

"Ha ha, very funny motherfucker." Mustard hinted.

"Well, what would you prefer? *I Want to Hold Your Hand? All You Need is Love? Sgt Mustard's Lonely Hearts Club Band?* Alright, I'll *Let It Be.* I'm on fire tonight!"

After pre-partying to the point at which our blood alcohol was enough to make our blood flammable, we stumbled down to our favorite watering hole, James Joyce. It was a dimly lit pub run by a couple Italians with limited English. One of the great attractions of the joint was this 5-liter glass you could order beer in. The glass looked as though it were a normal pint glass 10 times the scale. The glass absolutely dwarfed the person drinking it. Each person appeared like a baby trying to drink from a cup he wasn't supposed to. We would order 9.9% beer, aptly titled "Super Storm" and pass it around in a group of four. The last liter was always the most difficult, because the beer was coming all at once or not at all. I wonder how a beer soaked shirt collar affected my chances with the ladies on one of those nights.

"*What? I'm not sweating. Oh that. That's beer I spilled on myself. When you get to the end of the glass it just comes right at you! Where are you going? You gonna get your friends?*"

In the full swing of the night, I observed a rather bizarre sight. We were all pretty blasted at this point, but Mustard had somehow pulled ahead from the group. Sitting next to me, he began talking somewhat incoherently; like an Irishman eating a banana. He turned to Maria, a cute Latina girl sitting next to him. "Gur luck great. Ay dike ya, du ike me?"

Maria squinted at Mustard in confusion, which Mustard obviously misinterpreted as an act of seduction, as he immediately opened his mouth, protruded his tongue and dove in for the kiss. It was in awkward slow motion, like a sloth moving in to get nectar from an extended branch.

"Kevin WHAT are you doing?!" Maria blurted out before he quite reached her face.

Sitting up straight it took Mustard a second for the rejection to sit in. He tried to mumble something, but realizing that his words were essentially worthless, he simply began shoving her in the chest with one hand. "Kevin what's wrong with you?" Maria looked to me in fright.

"Alright Kevin, let's go have a *cigarette*. You want to have a *cigarette* Kevin?"

I helped Mustard to his feet and he followed me towards the bar's exit. I realized quickly that Mustard's feet were working about as well as his verbal skills. Exiting the bar became a pinball machine with Mustard as the ball, hitting every group of Italian men and bouncing off them, while I ran damage control. "What's dur provlem!" Mustard would slur.

"Ah, *scusa*, my friend is *ubriaco perso. Canadese*, eh."

When we finally made it outside, I leaned Mustard against a construction fence with 2 cars in front of him to cushion any kind of fall he might take. I lit us each a cigarette and pretended to know exactly what he was mumbling.

"Blurbidy du-bop. Day day dum."

"Yeah, I know right?"

Then it happened. Somehow, some way, Mustard leaned forward and fell. Not on me in front of him, not on the construction fence supporting him, not on the cars on either side, but somehow making a 90 degree pirouette right in between the car and the fence, he did a perfect tree fall on his face. Standing over him I sat him up.

"How'm I doing?" Mustard said as he flung his head back.

Blood was trickling down the center of his face. His forehead was cut, nose broken and lip busted. I immediately sobered up.

"Oh, not *that* bad. Just a little… we should get you outta here."

I helped him to his feet, put his arm around me and walked him over to the window of the bar. I banged on the glass and motioned to the bartender to come to the door. He came over and seeing the gruesome sight, ran over to my friends who had been continuing the evening inside. The boys hadn't missed a beat, while passing the 5-liter glass back and forth they had initiated a conversation with a group of beautiful Italian women.

The bartender alerted them. "Your friend is hurt in the face. Come now!"

My friends, realizing the urgency of the situation sprung into action. A plan was formed. One of them would get the girls' numbers while the other two chugged the last liters of beer.

What a plan. I mean how stereotypical of a male plan is that? "Someone is in trouble? We gotta prioritize this… you get the beer, I'll get the women, and then we'll help our friend."

I guess you can't blame these guys, they didn't know the magnitude of the situation. Heck, I'm sure even Batman had his off days. There must have been at least one time that some clown faced schmuck was terrorizing Gotham and Bruce Wayne didn't leave the party.

"The Penguin took over the zoo? You want me to get dressed for this? Fuck it, I'm finishing my champagne. For Christ's sake he's a penguin, and the zoo quite literally *is* a jail for animals. Justice served. Now if you don't mind Alfred, I got a chick here who's wearing nothin' but my utility belt. Gotta go!" [Click]

The bartender returned and pulled the glass from Charlie's lips. "Your friend bleeding out his face."

My friends made it outside just in time for Mustard to lose consciousness. We decided to carry him 8 blocks to the nondescript hospital, which happened to be kiddy-corner from our apartment building. When I originally arrived in my neighborhood I didn't know it was a hospital and I was hesitant about taking Mustard there. First impressions can really mess you up. It's interesting what you will infer while living in a new country, the assumptions and leaps of logic your mind will make in order to fit the puzzle pieces together. When first moving into my neighborhood, I immediately noticed what appeared to be gay pride flags with the word "Pace" written on them and the multitude of Italians with bandaged faces. In order to explain this, my mind had me convinced that I had just moved to the gay neighborhood and that a large percentage of Italians had eye problems. It took me 3 weeks to find out that they were in fact rainbow striped "peace" flags and that I lived directly across the street from a hospital.

It would be an understatement to say that I was still a little apprehensive about taking him there. Every single patient that wandered out of the hospital had either a leg cast or one of these massive eye patches. Every single one. Using my powers of deduction I could only come up with a couple scenarios in which this was possible.

At first I made the assumption that Italian doctors treated each malady with either an eye patch or a leg cast.

"You have back problems? Take an eye patch and call me in two days."

or

"This foot cast should stop the bleeding."

I then started wondering if perhaps there was a clumsy doctor with a hook for a hand dangerously strolling through the halls talking with big Italian arm gestures.

Scared that either of these two situations were possible, I had spent the first 3 months living in Italy rehearsing the phrase "Don't take me to the hospital, take me to the embassy."

After lugging Mustard into the hospital, the doctors informed us that it was in fact a foot and eye hospital. They were going to call an ambulance to take Mustard to the hospital across town.

While we were waiting I began to think about the concept of a foot and eye hospital. What a strange combination.

"Sorry we can't help you here, we're just foot and eye doctors. You need to take this note and go down the street to the ass and mouth hospital."

When would the combination come in handy?

"I got poked in the eye and twisted my ankle."

"Boy, did you came to the right place."

Returning from the hospital, I opened the medieval doors to the apartment building. The faint noise of music, that I could only assume came from my apartment 5 stories above, echoed down the staircase of the building. After climbing the 5 levels of stairs, and with my bloody shirt over my shoulder, I kicked open the door to the apartment. There was Charlie and Maria singing *La Bamba*, at full volume, in Spanish. Charlie paused momentarily.

"Hey you're back man... *La La, La La Bamba neccesito, un poco de gracias, arrrrrriba!*"

The next morning Geraldo woke me up at 9 a.m. to go check on Mustard at the hospital across town. After riding a bus for 45 minutes, which didn't help the hangover I was fighting off, we arrived. Stepping up to the information desk I told the administrator that we were there to see Kevin Mustard. She looked through a couple of pages of names and said that there was no one with that name on the list.

I asked her to check again. Nothing.

Confused, I was about to leave when I had an idea.

"How about – *Kay- veen –Moose- tard.*"

"*Oh si! Kayveen Moosetard*, down the hall, waiting room C."

When I got to waiting room C, I saw a doctor who politely escorted me to a hallway where he was being kept.

Mustard was in a full neck brace and with his nose bandaged, handcuffed to a stretcher on rollers. The doctor ensured me that, "the handcuffs and stretcher are a precaution so that he doesn't hurt himself. He is still inebriated and was acting a little crazy earlier. Now I must fill out a report on your friend. How was he attacked?"

"Excuse me?"

"He said that he was attacked by a gang of Moroccans."

I tried to hold back a smile. Right at that time a beautiful Italian nurse went to Mustard's side to check on him. Of course. I mean what would you say? What was he supposed to say to a beautiful nurse? How could he tell the truth?

Should he try to play it off casually "Let's just say... I'm not the best stand-er."

Was he supposed to be literal – "Who'd I get into a fight with? The ground."

"What's the best way to put this? The world was spinning and I decided to stop it – with my face."

I wanted to tell them "I could tell you who attacked him. I've had run-ins with this troublesome bunch before. There were three of them who attacked him at the bar: Jack Daniels, Johnnie Walker and one they simply referred to as *the Jaeger–meister*."

I fought back the jokes and told the doctor the truth, "he fell on his face."

The doctor looked at me strange. "That's it? By himself, he fell on his face? Are you sure?"

That is when Mustard tried to make an escape.

Still handcuffed to the stretcher with his neck

brace on, from a half-laying half-sitting up position, he attempted to pump his way out of the hospital. The doctor looked back at me in recognition, filled out the accident report and left. Mustard, obviously disoriented, carried on with his escape for the next 2 hours. He looked like one of those 2 man railroad pump handcarts, squeaking and see-sawing his way down the hall of the hospital, until a passing nurse would notice he had moved and gently push him back to his starting position. He was relentless.

Skeeker, skeeker, skeeker...
Skeeker, skeeker, skeeker...
Nurse rolling him back.

The doctor returned and told me that it would be another hour or two until they set his nose, so I got on a bus and headed home.

During the bus ride, I replayed the film reel from the night before in my mind: the board game, the night at the bar, Maria's rejection and of course the fall.

I felt bad for the guy. A night that started out with promise of conquering the world, ended with the world punching him in the nose. Although Kevin had set out to play a game of Risk that night, he ended up playing a game of Clue. And nobody would have guessed the cards that would be dealt: Sgt. Mustard, in the street, with a bottle of Jaeger.

Tequila Suicides

I had just made the journey across town to a supermarket where one could procure the proper supplies. We had been in Italy for a few months and people had been growing a bit homesick, so we came up with the idea of throwing an *aperitivo*, but with American food as the appetizers.

Whenever I am abroad I realize that the stereotypes of Americans are pretty set in stone and I try to do all I can to refute them, *no matter how accurate they may be*. This keeps me pretty busy, as I feel much less like an ambassador for my country and more like a PR specialist running damage control.

As I got on the bus and grabbed the rail, I was careful to hold my shopping bags tightly. All I needed was for one of the bags to fall open, some hot dogs hit the floor, a jar of peanut butter to roll the length of the bus, and my cover would be blown.

Bibbidy-bappy badaba-buppy. I-a knew it! All these fat-ass Yankee bastards. They can't help themselves, it's just mangia mangia mangia all the time.

I found myself in a vulnerable position when I was suddenly compromised from across the bus.

"Hey Mike! Ciao amico!"

It was Dave, our program's own walking, talking American stereotype. I gave him a nod, hoping that would be enough so that he wouldn't yell more half-assed Italian across a bus completely packed with native speakers. Dave was a good guy, a nice guy, but not exactly a Rhodes Scholar, more like the village idiot that somehow was able to navigate through the process of getting his passport. When abroad it made you cringe sometimes knowing that he was helping to mold the view of what an American was. Dave spoke with his mouth wide open, like a novelty wall-mountable singing bass. I didn't press the button, but the fish kept talking.

"Yo…andare …umm…Sicily."

Literal Translation: I [in Spanish] to go [in Italian] Sicily [in English]

Just brilliant. In an attempt to show all Americans weren't as stupid as the ones seen nightly on the TV show Cops, I responded in my best Italian.

"*Cosa hai detto? Tu andrai a Sicilia, e perche? Cosa farrai di la?*"

"Umm, what? Yeah… si, Sicilia. I'm going there…"

I winced and waved Dave over to end the spectacle. Dave had a way of making things awkward in public situations. He didn't do it on purpose, he just couldn't help himself.

A month previously we had gone to a fancy restaurant for Franklin's birthday. Dave started singing happy birthday in Italian, only Dave doesn't know Italian or the Italian Happy Birthday song. So during the birthday dinner, as the maître d' personally lit the candles at our table, Dave improvised a version that mixed in some of the lyrics from a classic Mexican holiday song. Dave sang three choruses, all by himself, at full volume.

"Feliz compleano – oh –oh Feliz compleano – oh –oh."

Our friend Jacob had been going on a bunch of

weekend trips with Dave around that time, which made me ask Jacob how he could spend so much time with Dave.

"I don't know. There is something about him that only the beast inside of me can appreciate. That kid is like a social savant, he has no filter and he goes for it even when he has no idea what he is doing. One day he may make an ass out of himself buying a train ticket and another day he convinces two gorgeous chicks to come party with us on the Riviera. He's able to do it all because he has no idea what is going on and doesn't care."

Jacob didn't spend time judging Dave or avoiding him in group situations, he would bring him along and enjoy watching him interact with the world.

"He's fucking hilarious, it's like watching a baby giraffe learn to walk for the first time. I feel like I'm in the movie *Rainman*. I'm Tom Cruise, he's Dustin Hoffman, I bring him along and cash in on his natural brilliance."

Back on the bus Dave continued his verbal diarrhea.

"I thought I would go down to Sicily next week for Thanksgiving. I bet they make the best food for Thanksgiving."

"Uh, Dave, Italians don't celebrate Thanksgiving."

"What? Seriously? Why not?"

"Well for starters the Mayflower landed in Plymouth not Palermo."

"Ah shit, all the Indians and everything. Well I bet you they will still have some bomb food down there. Right?"

"They probably do. Where are you off to right now?"

"I'm going to your place, Jacob told me he had some news and we are smoking cigars."

We really should have customs agents that interview our citizens before they go abroad.

"Ok, and what is the purpose of your trip?"

"I'm going to Paris to celebrate the 4th of July."

"Could you please step over here sir? I'll just hold on to this passport for you."

When we arrived at the apartment people were already there, plates were getting prepared, wine was uncorked and beers were being cracked. Jacob arrived with a box of cigars that he passed around. He had just become an uncle. Dave asked him how.

Jacob was 27 years old, but looked in his mid

thirties and like he just got off a decade long tour with Keith Richards. His skin was pale; his eyes were swollen and underlined with dark rings from relentless partying. I've never seen anyone sweat from their eyelids, until I met Jacob. His smile had a mischievous look as if preceded by the words 'do you dare me?'

His ruthless partying had also affected his mind. More often than not his brain would skip like a scratched CD. He would be mid-sentence beginning a thought and then just lose it completely, like someone trying to recall a dream from the night before. Many times this would happen when he had drawn the whole room's attention. He would cut into a conversation and begin a compelling thought – "You know the interesting thing about dating a German woman is that ahhh... Ahhhhhhhhh." He would squint in one last attempt to grasp the fading thought, look around the room at each of us hanging on to the conclusion and then shrug, throw back his head and let out a raspy laugh. The most common response was to give him a worried look, then join in on the laughter. Always followed by the thought: *Good god man you gotta take a break every now and then.*

Everyone was abroad looking for an escape, but I'm pretty sure Jacob had already gagged the guards, chiseled the vent, dug the tunnel, scaled the fence, sawed through the barbed wire, met his accomplice and was living under an assumed identity.

Two hours later the night was in raging climax; empty bottles and full belly laughs filled the apartment. A cute redhead named Chelsea with purple lips from all the chianti she had sucked down, roamed the party asking each person if they had tried her cookies. Jacob just sat chain smoking and chewing on ice in the corner.

"You guys want to get some hash?"

Franklin looked up immediately as if Jacob had just solved one of life's great mysteries.

"You can get hash?"

"Oh yeah. There are tons of hidden places, you just have to know the right spot."

Charlie cut in comical exuberance "Well then let's go."

In order to get hash we would have to leave the party; only we were the hosts of the party. To make it work we would have to bring everyone with us. We discovered Jacob's car did not have enough seats for everyone, so we did the sensible thing and piled in like the circus clowns we were at that point.

Jacob started the adventure by peeling out and screaming through a yellow light at the intersection. He was weaving through traffic and accelerating whenever he had space like he was in some kind of wild car chase. I was unsure if we were chasing or being chased, but the uncomfortable laughs grew more and more worried as the g-force threw people around in the car. I had to speak up.

"Hey ah, Jacob. Maybe slow, slow it down a bit. This isn't the Batmobile."

As soon as I said this, Jacob looked back at me with a grin more closely resembling the Joker. He jerked the wheel and the car jumped onto the sidewalk. It was a wide arch covered sidewalk with enough room for a newsstand, a few pedestrians and apparently a Fiat Punto. Bystanders jumped out of the way as everyone in the car let out a simultaneous scream. He rode to the end of the block and pulled back onto the road. He gave me another grin; I guess I was along for the ride.

"This park up here usually has some Moroccans that will have some hash."

The headlights lit up the empty park with one trail that led into the darkness. There was no one there. We thought that maybe we were out of luck when a man jumped up from behind a bush and made a giant one-armed wave and then went back to hiding. Jacob, Charlie and Franklin drunkenly interpreted this as subtle drug-dealer-code for an invitation and exited the car. I stayed behind with the 2 girls and a Dave.

As soon as they entered the park, the cops came in from all angles. The arm wave hadn't been an invitation at all, but a warning. I didn't know what to do. There were cops everywhere. So I sat there for the next ten minutes watching nervously as drunk girl Chelsea narrated the scene that was unfolding through the windshield.

"Oh my god, what are the cops doing here! That's craaazy. Oh wait, are we in trouble? Oh my god, those uniforms are so cute, they look like mailmen uniforms designed by Louis Vuitton. They're making them empty their pockets. Oh my god. Why is Jacob yelling in Italian and flashing his wallet like he works for the FBI? That's hilarious. Did you, hey Mike, hey Mike did you try my cookies?"

I felt like I was baby sitting "Yeah they were great."

Dave turned and looked at me, his eyes growing with a thought.

"Wouldn't it be so cool if we were on the Italian version of cops. *Bad boys bad boys che cazzo fai, che cazzo fai when they come for you.*"

A cop approached the window, scanning the car and sizing us up with his flashlight. Right when he got close Chelsea stuck her head out the window.

"I make the best cookieees. Do you know... Do you like cookies? You are cute. You would totally eat my cookies."

And then it was over. Somehow, someway, they decided that we were allowed to leave. We left and went to the first bar we could find.

"You guys want a shot?"

"Well, why not? What are we having?"

"Tequila Suicides!" Jacob said slapping his cash on the bar and hollering at the bar tender. "Four tequilas!"

Jacob looked back at us with that wild smile of his, as the bartender provided salt, cut limes and poured up four oversized shots of tequila. I thought it was going to be a normal tequila shot, the whole lick-the-back-of-your-hand, salt, tequila and lime gig, until Jacob started chopping up the salt on the bar with his credit card and the bar tender handed us four straws that had just been cut in half.

"You guys ready? Follow my lead." Jacob let out a breath and in a swift motion sniffed the salt off the bar with his straw, took down the tequila in one slug, tipped his head back and began squeezing the lime directly into his eyes.   Jacob gave out a *woot* as he struggled with the pain he had just inflicted on himself. He looked like he had just been punched in the nose and kicked in the crotch at the same time, which was a hilarious sight until we realized that we were next in line.

"Alright guys," Jacob choked out while still reeling from the shot.

Franklin shrugged. "Well fuck, here goes nothing."

We all followed right behind him, salt, tequila and lime.

"Keep your eyes open," Jacob yelled, as lime squirted directly into our eyes.

Right after the shot your whole face was on fire. We bobbed and weaved in pain, all four of us pounding the bar, hollering, laughing, and cussing. The bartender handed me a glass of water and when I was finally able to squint my eye open, I realized that we had become the center of attention; four obnoxious, loud, binge-drinking, cussing Americans. I recounted the night – driving on the sidewalk, almost getting arrested, incapacitating ourselves with Tequila suicides. Why did I hang out with Jacob? This guy, this eye-sweating, joy-riding, trouble-seeking degenerate fucking guy? I don't know. All I can tell you is that there's just something about him that only the beast inside me can appreciate.

Trick or Treat

It was late October and I was in a funk. I had a strange itch in my soul. An overwhelming melancholy; call it culture shock, call it homesickness, or maybe just a depletion of endorphins from too much fun in such a short time span. Until a week before I had been living out *La Dolce Vita*; a real life Marcello Mastroianni with inner suave, outward cool and seemingly always surrounded by the party.

I began sneaking away and taking walks by myself to Parco Vittorio late in the afternoon. Sitting on a park bench I would wait for the early evening to cool the noise of the city. Staring up at the brilliant colors in the ocean of trees I would watch as gusts of wind pushed waves of leaves, sending them fluttering down like metallic confetti, flickering with the reflected light of the setting sun like embers from a smoldering fire, as they burst from their branches burning bright before extinguishing their glow and settling into the shade.

I would light a cigarette and just let my mind go. The worst part about this feeling in my gut was that I couldn't really explain it even to myself, let alone those around me. I couldn't find my bearings. Maybe it's the feeling of being stuck in between the present and the past, your home and your once-imagined-dream-life, and the realization that maybe you have no country at all.

On one particular afternoon I returned from one of my solo trips to find everyone in the house in frenzied preparation. I had not only completely forgotten about the party that we were going to that night, but had even forgotten that it was Halloween. Maybe this is just what I needed, a good old American style holiday to quench my ache for familiarity.

Charlie and Franklin greeted me with the sympathy that can be expected from your male companions. I passed Franklin in the hallway on my way in.

"How was the pity party bro?"

Charlie gave a chuckle from the bathroom and poked his head out.

"You remember to stop by the store on your way back?"

41

"For what?"

"Pick up a pair of testicles?"

As I bowed my head and sighed, Franklin gave me a good hard couple pats on the back, male code for: *Just messing with you, little serious, I did mean what I said, you do need to smile and stop being such a pussy, but it was also a joke.*

My brother wasn't one to see me moping around the house, so he kept going in an effort to cheer me up.

"I'd give you some of my Prozac but I just chopped it up and freebased it about an hour ago. Sorry you're feeling bad... God, I feel great!"

If something didn't work he would just keep going. He was never afraid to go with the lowbrow humor to cheer me up.

"What's wrong? You poo? You poop? You poop in your pants? You got poo-poo pants?"

That one got me. Don't know why. Just the ridiculousness of it, which was perhaps best for all of us, because knowing my brother, his next act was probably going to be coming out of the bathroom wearing nothing but a towel around his waist, walking like a centaur and speaking in a deep lispy voice.

"Mike, now I don't want you to be alarmed, but I've made a pretty big change... Gone through a transformation of sorts… Got some work did."

Dropping the towel to the floor, he has tucked his junk back between his legs displaying his newly made mangina.

"Say hello to your new sister!"

And you better like that one, or he will spin around and ask if you have seen his fruit-basket anywhere.

Not having prepared beforehand I went straight back out the door and down the street hoping to find a store that could offer me something that resembled a costume.

It didn't feel like it was Halloween; there were no pumpkins, no cobwebs, no orange and no black. The only sign that it was Halloween was the handful of children that were quietly moving from store to store to get candy.

Halloween still being pretty new to the country, they had decided to cut out the middleman and instead of people going to the store, buying candy, bringing it home and passing it out to children, they just go straight to the source, store to store getting candy handed out to them. I thought it was a gyp, little mafiosos shaking down their local grocery stores.

"Hey ah, looks like a dangerous neighborhood you got here, especially with all these ghosts and goblins running around... I don't know if just one gumdrop is gonna do it. That's better... Glad we could come to an understanding. Happy Halloween..."

After rounding a corner I came across a hardware store. I grabbed a reflector jacket, a hard hat and some gloves. *I'll be a construction worker.* That's not really a costume though, but more of an outfit. A costume like so many other things needs that extra level to be good. You need a spin to your costume. I could be a zombie construction worker – just walk around with my arms out, drooping my mouth and looking like an idiot, but everyone would probably just think I got a head start drinking. I could be a stripper construction worker – just buy everything two sizes too small. I decided to go with the obese construction worker. The old trick of shoving a pillow in my shirt. Bam, I had a costume.

When I got back up to the apartment Franklin was busy primping his costume and applying children's makeup to his forehead. He was playing a superhero villain that was popular at the time with a bullseye on his head. Charlie was desperately trying to put together household items to make his costume as he had just spent most his cash for the month on booze in recent nights. He was stuck in the same dilemma I was; an outfit that wasn't quite a costume yet. With just an over-sized cheap raincoat and a chimneysweep style hat – he was a fisherman, but needed to steal some face paint from Franklin to make dark rings around his eyes so he could be a *dead* fisherman.

Right before we left I could sense that the guys were still a little on edge about taking me out. I was a liability. Nobody really wants to take Salty Susan out on the town with them. My brother gave me one last pep talk and Franklin poured shots while keeping eye contact.

"Cheer up Meekster. We're gonna get you a lady tonight. Laid by a lady and it's going to be kind of difficult if you are anchoring the table at the party."

Sticking his fists under his shirt and doing a chick voice, "*Hey, I thought I would come over to the more subdued side of the room. Who's your mute friend and why is he weeping?*"

"We need you to… how do you say… Cheer up bucko!"

We walked the path to some American girls' place for

a little pre-party.   Pedestrians on the street were doing double takes as we passed by them on the sidewalk. I was unsure just what they were looking at, if it was our lack of style or if they were just wondering what the hell these three characters were doing together.   Come to think of it, they were probably just making sure that the tattoo on Franklin's forehead wasn't a swastika.

I felt like a goof in my costume. It didn't feel like Halloween. It was missing an essence, the thing that makes it come alive. Halloween was about getting on a disguise and losing yourself in a character. It was about fear. It was supposed to be scary. I know that most of the time people just do cheesy things to give the Rated-G version of scary, but there was a sense of earnestness about it.   The rustling fall leaves, the candlelight illuminating demon faced pumpkins, the person in the shadows covered in fake blood that you think for just a moment might be real.

As we showed up at the apartment the two American girls and their roommate were in full Halloween garb with drinks in their hands. They were dressed as a French Maid, a Sexy Devil and this takes the cake, Lucie– Lucie was dressed as Little Red Riding Hood. I heard *Werewolves of London* echoing in my head.

As they stood across from us it was a classic Halloween moment. The three girls dressed as man's fantasies in the flesh while we stood across from them: a fat guy, a dead guy and a dude with a face tattoo.

A few laughs and a couple drinks downed, and we were on a bus to the costume party. Franklin did gainers on the bus using the handrails and I sat in the back. Lucie came over and talked to me for a while, but I just sat there, tongue tied like a middle-school-dance-wallflower. She quickly bored and went to the front of the bus for more excitement.

In the vacuum of her exit Charlie and Franklin stumbled over.

Charlie - Talking to Lucie bro?

Franklin - Yeah, I'm just waiting for her to do the whole – 'what a deep voice you have, what big eyes you have' gig and hopefully notice the bulge in my pants. Sha-wing!

Mike - Not if I get there first.

Franklin - Oh a little competition? Well you want to back flip for it?

Franklin got a running start and did another gainer using the handrails as the bus driver looked in his rear mirror with a scowling glare.

47

At the party all of the costumes were interesting, but a little unsettling. There was an Italian Dracula, a Romanian Bullfighter and a Spanish Gondolier. I found it a bit strange; it was like they played stereotype musical chairs. There were also Germans in the living room dressed as a witch and Robin Hood, looking as though they came straight out of *The Brothers Grimm*. The Swedes and the Spanish had no costumes at all. The Russian soldier by the bathroom was a little unnerving. Oh, and there was a Mexican Batman taking tequila shots in the kitchen.

I could take you through the evening, but I thought I would spare with a brief synopsis:

Franklin in full form, bouncing around from girl to girl running lines from movies.

Me at the alcohol infused punch bowl.

Charlie in full tilt breathing life into the party with wild antics and slapstick style comedy.

Me sneaking a shot by myself in the kitchen.

A very drunk Italian Dracula exiting the bathroom with his cape backwards, covered in the remnants of the wine he drank earlier and the spaghetti he had for dinner. Strangely enough it just made his costume look more authentic.

Me, the punch bowl is now empty.

Drunk Mexican Batman passed out in the bathtub.

I guess Gotham is in for it tonight.

I finally decided to go in search of Lucie hoping to build up some nerve and redeem myself from earlier. Take a chance. Give one of those sad, drunk, desperate-flailing attempts at romance that will hopefully come off as cute in some way.

I immediately found her when I went out for a cigarette; she was down a flight of stairs, making out with Franklin. The wolf found it's prey and the lumberjack was nowhere to be found.

My brother, noticing I had exited, joined me at the doorway.

"The Spanish guys are rolling to a Eurasmus party. Let's go!"

We went to a club downtown and I had forgotten that we were pretty much the only ones celebrating Halloween. My hardhat and reflector vest shined bright in the black lights on the way in. I tried to blend in, feeling uncomfortable as my fat suit kept pushing its way through the crowd. A couple of *Cuba Libres* later YMCA comes on and I suddenly became a star and a mascot. Pulled on stage, I played up my character dancing with a fat girl and belly bumping with authority.

When things wound down Charlie and I started the long walk home. There is something amazingly pleasant about walking the big empty city streets in the wee hours of the morning. There was not a soul in sight and we could only hear our footsteps, the dripping of rain from the gutters and the rushing of cars somewhere off in the distance.

We walked for about an hour using the tallest buildings as a rough guide, the way you do in big cities; using the *Mole*, the *Duomo*, the *Castello* to find our way. When we got stuck in an area where the surrounding buildings were too large to find our way we decided we should ask the next human being we saw for some help.

A beautiful woman exited some giant apartment doors down the block and across the street. She was making her way to her car when Charlie ran over to ask directions. Given that he had spoken English all night and drank enough to kill a Mexican Batman, Charlie's Italian was butchered but understandable.

The woman let out a muffled shriek and quickened her pace; her heals clacking at an uneasy rhythm. When she made it to her car door she began stabbing at it with her key, frantically trying to find the keyhole.

Watching from the darkness across the street it was clear she was overreacting to someone asking for directions.

In my mind I was about to write her off as rude, inconsiderate, unwilling to help a foreigner, overreacting to perceived fears from embellished nightly news reports – when I realized what was really going on. I burst into laughter, unable to control myself, tears streaming down my cheeks as her car screeched and she sped down the empty street to leave Charlie dumbfounded on the sidewalk with his hands extended.

This finely dressed beauty, fresh and floating from a magic evening, a chance encounter, a romantic dinner, skips down the stairs of her lovers building.

As she exits: The world outside has changed, it's grown dark, it's rained, water falls from the gutters in hollow drips, the street empty and lifeless. Right as the large medieval doors slam and lock behind her, a figure emerges out of the pitch black stumbling directly at her. Its clothes are tattered, its cheeks are pale and eyes sunken surrounded by dark rings. It's a DEAD…VAMPIRE…FISHERMAN…ZOMBIE.

The dead-vampire-fisherman-zombie yells out in slurred speech.

"Hey I'm not from here. I'm not alive. I need

your help. Help me find a home. I'm not alive here. Don't run!"

As she gets to her car and struggles to get her key in the lock, she hears from the darkness a deep evil laugh that echoes off of each building.

And that was the end of the melancholy. My brother and I laughed the whole way home and it released whatever knot that had been tied in my stomach. The poor girl had no idea it was Halloween, but for me she made Halloween complete.

One Bus Stop, Three Blocks and a New Pair of Pants

I felt the warmth from a streak of sun hitting my cheek. Apparently it was already morning. Rubbing my face with both hands I used all my strength to focus before I could open my eyes. The light was streaming through the window across the red Italian tiles of buildings in the distance. The opera sounds of the Italian morning rose from the street below; shopkeepers opening their storefronts, Vespas accelerating, neighbors yelling at each other.

I tried to orient myself. Is this my – yes it is my room – *I live in an Italian apartment – but how the hell did I get here? It was a miracle! I had made it to my bed.* Somehow despite everything, just as my world had been knocked off its axis, I managed to find my way across the city and to my bed.

I wanted to give myself a high five. I don't know where 'wanting to high five yourself for making it to your bed after an alcohol infused night' falls on the problem drinker scale, but I imagine it probably lands somewhere between having a bottle of wine with lunch and blacking out at your nephew's birthday party.

"Lil Mike bro, you're going to be late."

Franklin tossed me a cigarette and placed coffee in my hands. I stumbled out of bed with a swig of coffee and went over to the kitchen sink. As I splashed cold water on my face, puzzle pieces of the night before began to fall into place. The Polaroid picture memories of the night out came back in still images, before becoming brief flashes of film with choppy cuts.

We'd met at our apartment. It was a lively Tuesday night with everyone in our building meeting at our place for some cocktails before hitting the town. I had a few drinks at the house, maybe 2, no 3, no 4, and then decided to crack some champagne and take it with me on the bus despite some disapproving looks from the locals. This explains the rocket ship blast in memory from my house to the bar. At the

pub: 1 pint, 2 pints, this place serves liters? Shots.
Oh the fucking shots. And the mystery of why I can
hear my heartbeat its metronome in the veins of my
forehead has just been solved.

Immediately a panic came over me and I checked my
pants for my wallet like a guy in an action movie
checking to see if he'd been shot. It was there.
Sweet, I am on a roll.

But I felt some other odd object in my pocket,
rounder than a lighter. *Lipstick? Why do I have lipstick?*
It was like a movie, where a character awakens from a
dream and has a feather in his pocket and the whole
big cliché – it was real after all...

But as the reel began to play again in my head I
knew that last night hadn't been a dream come true.

Walking through the bar a few people were giving
me double takes, the quintessential and international
sign that your buzz has turned into a full-blown
drunk. I remember dancing, more drinks and
exchanging banter with the bartenders.

Then there was Lauren across the bar. She gave
me a playful stare and then slid her white-rimmed
Sofia Loren shades down over her eyes. She had
never looked so amazing, so glamorous. I didn't
know if it was just me or the 10 drinks, the bottle of

champagne and the shots of whiskey, but she looked like a movie star.

I walked smoothly and steadily around the bar without breaking my gaze. When I arrived at her side it was like she didn't see me. That's odd. We just had a moment. I'm always up for a little game of cat and mouse.

"How are you doing tonight?"

"Oh, hi." She swiveled her bar stool and sipped from the straw in her umbrella drink.

Playing hard to get huh?

I noticed that her purse lay open and just inside was her vibrant red movie star lipstick. Well let's see where this goes. With a blatantly obvious gesture I picked up the lipstick and put it in my pocket.

"Hey is that my lipstick? Did you just take my —"

"Oh is it? I don't think so. Do you also wear Endless Ruby Number 5?" I whispered as I did what I thought would be a hilarious hit, nonchalantly applying the lipstick broadly to my mouth and smacking my lips. She returned my glaze with a glare.

There is a splice in the movie here.
[Footage Not Found]

Her shades are off now and she is giggling at

something I said.

"Was that inappropriate?"

"No." She then squinted at me from an angle as her head tilted slightly forward. That's when I went in for the kiss, lipstick and all. I felt her hand on my chest, which I thought was a great sign until I realized that her elbow was locked and she was keeping me at bay. I opened my eyes to her cold smile, her eyebrows raised.

As I stumbled out of the situation I heard the gaggle of laughter and a big 8th grade teasing 'Oooooooh' from the Spanish girls standing just beyond my drunk bubble. The embarrassment of the moment burned on my cheeks and neck, the emotion forcing me to immediately judge the onlookers. Of course the Spanish chicks were entertained, what do you expect from a culture that considers bullfighting an art form? Here they were spectators to an over-dressed, Capri-wearing, pretentious-bourgeois, engaged in a cowardly, sadistic tradition of slowly torturing, humiliating, and finally terminating a terrified, confused, maimed, psychologically tormented, and physically debilitated animal, who desperately seeks his escape amid the pomp and pageantry of unashamed people who applaud the— you get the idea, these girls were being total skanks.

Jacob swooped in out of nowhere, threw his arm over my shoulder and guided me out of the situation.

"Two shots."

Jacob gave me a wild smile as the bar tender passed us our shots.

"At least you went for it. To going for it."

We clinked glasses.

```
Fade to black
```

```
Cut to: Internal Bedroom
A young American is slouching over the
kitchen sink with one eye open and takes
another sip of his black coffee.    His
roommates look on with a look of pity on
their faces.
```

"Rough night last night, huh bud?" Franklin turned to Charlie. "He tried to make out with Lauren last night and got rejected. Hard."

"Oh that sucks."

They knew as well as I did that the university gossip was far worse than freaking high school. Not only had I spoiled my chances with Lauren but also with her 5 roommates, not to mention the lovely Spanish girls who watched me charge in for the kill only to get the bullfighters cape and a spirited *Ole*. By the time I got to school that day the account would have probably already made its full rounds.

The coffee worked wonders and as I lit a cigarette and waited for the bus I was amazed at how great I felt, at least physically, after consuming such a massive amount of booze. I felt outstanding. Just had to go on this 45 minute bus ride, knock out an hour of class, avoid some of the gossip queens at the school and I'm good on the day. Right at this point my stomach gurgled and shifted. It felt buoyant.

As I stepped on the bus I felt something get away, how do you say this? I felt a light pocket of air escape my... I passed.... I farted, alright. I didn't mean to do it while I was just getting on the bus, I'm not a jerk, I just took a big step and it snuck out. I immediately saw an open spot and flopped into the seat only to find my situation a lot worse than I previously thought. *There is just the lightest bit of dampness where I'm sitting and my seat is bone dry...* That's right, I just sharted. Brilliant. As I pondered what this means to my morning the bus began to pull out.

The engines started to vibrate gently. My stomach

gurgled again. Suddenly it felt like the growing slime from *Ghostbusters* angrily expanding inside me. I was in a bit of trouble, as it appears that what I had just experienced was just a preview, a warning.

Right when my inner motivational speaker states 'maybe this will pass' – we hit a pothole, the bus changes gears and makes its first turn. My muscles clinch and hold on for dear life.

I'm not going to make it.

This bus is the absolute worst place I can be. The rumbling, the tremors, the aftershocks. Oh god. I feel as though I may just have a reverse volcano eruption in my pants.

The doors open at the first stop 3 blocks later. A bus stop I always felt was utterly useless, as you could literally see it from the previous bus stop, but I now realized why this bus stop was so pivotal. I make a mental note to write a letter to the city planning office thanking them.

In quick pencil leg movements I make it to the door and gingerly dismount. I look down the street and can see the sign of the bakery on the corner of my building just four blocks away. The four blocks seem to stretch for miles in the distance as my stomach growls once more. Knowing that time is of the essence, I start to march. Well maybe 'march' is an overstatement, I begin to waddle, like a penguin, with a torn hamstring.

A violent churn in my stomach convinces me once more that I'm not going to make it. Plan B. I desperately search for a plan B. As my gaze spins 360 degrees, I realize my bathroom options are not just limited, but nonexistent. Closest to me there is a restaurant that has one sign hanging in the window reading 'Dinner' and another reading 'Chiuso,' meaning closed. A cell phone shop – nope, a supermarket – chiuso, a construction site, a hair salon and a clothing store, then a slew of shops and cafes that should have bathrooms, but all chiuso chiuso chiuso. Damn Italians and their leisurely life, don't they know us Americans have shit to do?

Then I see it, not more than 10 steps to my left, a telephone booth. Plan C? It was probably the worst telephone booth for what my mind was desperately proposing as an emergency measure. The telephone booth was made of four crystal clear glass windows and probably the only thing in this city that wasn't covered in graffiti. It was positioned directly in between 2 walking paths. I stood for a moment at the door of the telephone booth and looked around. The busy city was crawling with people on their way to work; a sea of suits, briefcases, scarves and cigarettes. As I stood at that door I had the clarity of a life moment; a test of my character, will and morals.

Am I really going do this, right here in the middle of the street, in a glass phone booth? *Maybe I could fake like I'm just making a call...* But am I about to ruin a few dozen peoples mornings and one street cleaner's entire day? *Maybe I could act like I am just tying my shoe...* You know a spectator may just get an image that he can't shake; an image that will suddenly come to mind in the midst of a presentation or while talking to their boss.

I am dressed in a clearly American outfit, baseball cap and all; about to spoil my ambassador status when the pain subsides and the cramps cease. I feel like I could run right now, but I know that this is only momentary. My inner motivational speaker again gives me a pep talk and I am on my way towards my apartment like a clumsy person learning the steps to some type of tango.

About a block down I reach a traffic light and right when my anxiety peaks the light turns red and the green walk symbol flashes. Maybe there is a God, twisted sense of humor, but there. As I reach the safe side of the opposite sidewalk the pain sets in again. The next half block is an uncomfortable blur of memory, emphasis on - uncomfortable. Now I look like I'd been shot or maybe hit by a car, limping down the street with beads of sweat forming on my face.

An Italian stranger stops and looks concerned

"*Scusa, ma tutto a posto? Lei ha bisogno di aiuto?*"

He's asking me if I need help. *Ahhh yes,* but what am I supposed to say?

As a matter of fact dear sir, I am in need of aide, you wouldn't happen to have diapers in that briefcase of yours would ya?

Not only is this highly doubtful, but I am unsure I even know the formal conditional imperfect tense necessary to say this in Italian.

How do you tell a perfect stranger that you're about to shit yourself and what exactly can they do for you anyway? I felt like a hostage victim with a bomb strapped to his chest.

Get back! Everyone get back! This thing is going to blow!

There is no red wire to cut to defuse this bomb.

Could this guy help me? What would MacGyver do? James Bond would be more resourceful than this. I scramble in my mind to see if there is some way he could help me.

Here's the short list of what I come up with:

Bring me a tarp, a pressure washer and a new pair of pants.

Quick, I need a pop up tent, a bucket and some baby wipes.

Write this down, a wet suit, duct tape and some air freshener.

Alright, a smoke bomb, orange cones and a pair of running shoes.

All I need is a bottle of whiskey, rain-boots and a fake mustache.

I frantically shake my head and hope that he just thinks I am crazy as I shuffle on. The last blocks move quickly and the fresh hope I get when I reach the door of my building allows me to endure the 1930s elevator ride to my 5th floor apartment. When the door is thrown open I make a mad dash the last 10 waddles to the bathroom. I could hear Franklin and Charlie in the kitchen practicing for a verbal language exam. The answers to the many questions that they must have had just after the apartment door was flung open only shortly after I had departed for school is soon made obvious by the sound effects that follow:

A strange pitter-patter of feet.

A bathroom door slam.

A muffled curse.

A pregnant pause.

A toilet flush.

And the shower nozzle screech to full blast as the water pounds the bathtub floor.

As laughter echoed into the bathroom I knew I wouldn't need to explain myself. I finished my shower and dried off. When I started the washing machine the burst of laughter came back to full volume. It is strange how traumatic experiences can put things in perspective. Somehow this bowel movement had made the embarrassment of the night before easier to stomach.

And lucky for me this story was just between me, Charlie and Franklin, and whoever else was around at 3 a.m. on a Saturday night when the energy died down and there was a lull in the conversation:

"Mike, did you tell them about your bus trip?"

"What bus trip?"

"You know, THE bus trip."

"No, strangely enough it hasn't come up."

Of course this just piques our companions'

interest and Charlie starts in –

"Which bus was that again, was it the number 2?"

Franklin tries not to lose it as he keeps it going.

"Maybe the 1 and a half bus? Tell them about the phone booth."

"You know… wow it's getting late…"

"Oh come on Lil Mike."

"Tell us! Come on!"

"I don't know what bus they are talking about, but did I ever tell you about the time I put on lipstick and tried to force-kiss Lauren?"

The Three Musketeers

At 5 o'clock in the morning our four adventurers stumbled out of the pub. There was a certain excitement in the air as the glimmer of daybreak lit up the empty street. When they entered the apartment building, the four broke the silence with laughter despite themselves. All of them knew that they had not only salvaged the evening but had an amazing night; quite the feat considering that earlier in the day they faced what seemed to be certain defeat.

Sergio poured the last four drinks of the night, handed them out and raised his glass.

"A toast. To my brothers, all for one and one for all!"

It had been a running joke of sorts; referring to

ourselves as *The Three Musketeers*. It actually was a rather fitting analogy and as silly as it was, our personalities lined up quite well with the real musketeers.

Being 18 years old, overconfident and filled with boyish arrogance, I was the obvious choice for D'Artagnan. The others were constantly guiding me, encouraging me to try new things and laughing at my inexperienced blunders.

Our Italian friend Sergio was Athos. He was older than the rest of us and carried a wisdom and intellect, part from being at home in his own country and part from his Italian passion for literature and poetry. This knowledge that he had was put to great use as he served as our own personal Cyrano De Bergerac when we were exchanging messages with Italian women.

Sergio – What are you doing over here by yourself?

Mike – I'm finishing off a text to Laura.

Sergio – Give me your phone.

Mike – What is that?

Sergio – It is this first part, you say like a

gentleman that she shouldn't be sad and that you could make her feel better. Then this last part is Dante. *Quanto la cosa e piu perfetta, piu senta il bene, e cosi la doglienza.* It means eh 'The more a thing is perfect the more it feels pleasure and pain.'

Mike – That is genius dude, I'm using that.

Sergio – What are you doing? Why are you deleting the first part?

Mike – I can't write exactly this, my Italian isn't that good. I gotta fuck up the grammar just enough so she thinks I wrote it.

When we were putting the analogy together, Franklin had a Steve Buscemi 'Why do I have to be Mr. Pink?' moment when we told him he was Porthos.

"Tell me how it doesn't make sense? How are you not Porthos? Would you argue against your preference for fashionable clothes, love of wine or your fondness of women?"

"But Porthos is always played by the fat guy."

"Oh, there is another one; Porthos' vanity. And you can't argue, when you are on a bender you stuff your fucking face."

"Touché, fuck I'm Porthos."

And Charlie was very much Aramis. With a girlfriend back in the states he gave off a certain religious purity, a desire to remain unadulterated and loyal, trying to bury his love for women while he was unavoidably pursued by them. He claimed that he was just a musketeer temporarily in Italy but would return to his true calling of devoutness upon return to the states.

His apprehension to pursue women made him the perfect wingman. He was an absolute master. It was a spectacle to watch, like a professional athlete setting up the rest of the team to score.

If you liked a girl but didn't know quite what to say, he would talk you up. If your conversation was failing he would do something to become the butt of a joke. If you were trying to talk to a girl and there was a sleaze-bag trying to swoop he would run interference with whatever bullshit he could get the other guy excited about.

Charlie – Who are you looking at? The brunette over there with *Pepé Le Pew*? Follow me, we will run what I call the pick and roll.

Grabbing his glass and walking past the couple, he would stop suddenly and then begin talking to the guy from the side opposite the brunette.

"Is that a *Juventus* shirt, fuck yeah, great team. Soccer or I'm sorry *futbol* right! How about that game a few days ago... you know what? I'm buying you a drink."

As the girl rolled her eyes the opportunity was there to slide in and start up a conversation. It was magic.

Now I don't want you to get the wrong idea. We weren't the musketeers that serve duty, King and Country; our purpose was less noble. We more closely resembled the musketeers when they were 'on leave,' on vacation, usually located at the beginning of the story or buried somewhere in the middle when they had fallen out of favor with the aristocracy, when there were no battles to be won or justice to be served, and you could find the heroes fall-down-drunk at a bar, wooing intoxicating women and chasing their insatiable appetite for adventure. We weren't the stern soldiers serving the greater good, but the adventurers grabbing a fistful of the good life.

Nothing beats a good story and that was the pursuit on a nightly basis, when the sense of adventure was the only goal. *This is going to be amazing or hilarious*; if we had a mantra that would be it. What I did against all the odds or how I was a spectacular failure. It encouraged a bold edge and gave the appearance of confidence. If this isn't going to be romantic it will be fun. It bred a certain lightheartedness, a sense of freedom. If I don't get laid I still gotta at least leave with something funny to say.

We had a whole slew of successful campaigns; Southern belles with ruby lips, mysterious French girls in candlelight and stories of climbing out of a Spanish beauty's window at daybreak.

But for every stolen kiss, romantic encounter, triumphant walk home at first light; was an ill-worded pickup line, a botched seduction and an embarrassing attempt at a 3-way.

On the day in question we had much more of the latter.

D'Artagnan awoke in the morning to find his comrade Porthos face down on the floor in his boxer briefs, no pillow, surrounded by empty beer cans and an empty pizza box with knifes sticking out of it. No sooner had Porthos made it to his feet, then did he have two beers in hand, stabbing them each with a knife and the two of them proceeded to shotgun the beers at 9 a.m.

Porthos had gone out the night before with a maiden heralding from the village of Houston, Texas. Apparently the evening had not gone according to plan.

D'Artagnan – Rough night?
Porthos – Understatement of the year.

Porthos went on to recount the story of how he had acquired his wounded heart and convinced D'Artagnan to help him drink his way back to health. Soon after, Aramis arrived and joined in on the inebriation with jubilation.

The three then remembered that there was a gala on the other side of the apartment complex, an *aperitivo* filled with wine, food and beautiful women.

As Porthos put on his best outfit and Aramis shaved, D'Artagnan decided it would be pretty hilarious to just arrive in his undergarment; a pair of long johns that would be accessorized with an over-sized winter coat, a hat and a scarf.

When they arrived the party had not even begun. The morning drinking had caused the group to lose track of time as they showed up to an evening party in the afternoon. The host had gone out to gather more supplies and guide her guests back to her residence. The gang decided to settle in and enjoy themselves with the faire wenches that had been left behind to prepare for the gala.

It is unclear what gaiety ensued, but the moment the fun ended will forever be remembered. What happens next could be described as an ambush, although it is difficult to decipher who was ambushing whom.

When Lady Lauren arrived at her residence with her dinner guests, all dressed in full aristocratic attire with expensive bottles of wine in hand, they were exposed to quite the scene. D'Artagnan, at this point disrobed down to simply his undergarment, had very noticeably placed a piece of produce in his pants and was in some sort of lunging position. Aramis, was nowhere to be found although you could hear some noises of pleasure echoing through the bedroom wall, and Porthos was very noticeably alleviating himself to the street below through the railing of the fourth floor French balcony located in the kitchen.

Lady Lauren – What the fuck is going on?!
D'Artagnan – Hey you guys are here, alright!

Porthos – Ah shit, sorry this isn't what it looks like. Maybe it is. Give me a second.

Not knowing quite what to do and on the verge of tears and fury, Lady Lauren burst into her room for refuge. There was a moment of confusion in the chamber and then loud shouting.

"Oh my god what are you two doing on my fucking bed?!"

"It's my bed too."

"Yeah but you are on the top bunk. Put on a shirt."

The yelling in the bedroom continued as Aramis entered the room trying to straighten up his disheveled garments.

Aramis – Oh everyone is here. Hey guys. Eh…yeah.

D'Artagnan – Why were you peeing in the kitchen and why didn't you stop?

Porthos – Uh yeah stop, cause I can do that midstream. There is no way. What? Just shove it in my pants, and walk around the party with a giant round piss stain on my groin? And technically I wasn't peeing *IN* the kitchen.

D'Artagnan – Semantics.

Porthos – Look who's fucking talking? You still have a zucchini in your junk.

The quarrel continued in the other room as the aristocrats stared at our three heroes in both disbelief and scorn.

Aramis – I don't really know why she is so pissed. Didn't you get Lauren topless at one of our *aperitivos*?

Porthos – I tried to…

Lauren emerged from her bedroom in a rage and approached the three miscreants. Porthos zipping his pants, Aramis buttoning his shirt and D'Artagnan just standing there in his underwear with a zucchini in hand.

Everyone soon learned that the musketeers' version of an *aperitivo* was quite different from Lauren's.

Apparently her idea of an *aperitivo* involved friends coming over in their finest clothes, standing around with sophisticated postures, and not a scantily clad gentleman with a fake bulge in his pants, reaching for items on the highest shelf for comedic affect. Her vision of the gala involved good conversation and prolonged gazes, and not drunken philanderers stoofing her roommate on her bed. Apparently her *aperitivo* involved fine wine and cheeses, and not pissing cheap beer from the window adjacent to the dining area.

Right at that moment Athos rode gallantly into the situation with a charming smile and a bottle of wine. He used his suave and tact to soothe the broken princess as the other musketeers tiptoed their way out of the apartment.

"D'Artagnan, Porthos, Aramis let's go."

"What are you guys *The Three Musketeers* or something?"

"We've seen better days."

Our heroes retreated to their apartment to regroup. In a mirrored reflection of the preparations earlier in the day D'Artagnan got dressed, Porthos shaved, Athos shot-gunned a beer and Aramis relieved himself. The four descended to the street a more formidable group, leaving the misadventure behind. As they made it to the pub they had new life, a fresh night to be filled with unbridled banter, some undeserved luck, and perhaps a stolen kiss, a romantic encounter and a triumphant walk home at first light.

Amsterdam

On January 17th we arrived in Amsterdam. It was the peak of our trip both figuratively and literally. At this time in Amsterdam, weed was as plentiful as ever, the Van Gogh Museum had just finished renovations and mushrooms were still legal.

Unfortunately mushrooms are now illegal, which upset me when I first heard it, but the more I think about it, the more I see the possible downside to having people doing mushrooms in your city. It's quite understandable why you wouldn't want tourists ingesting mind-bending drugs then wandering your neighborhood. Nobody needs to take the first sip of their morning coffee, peer out the window, only to discover a foreigner having a full-on conversation with the garden gnome.

The last thing you need on the way to the grocery store is a run-in with somebody that thinks he *is* the Lord of the Rings.

"Look, here's the deal Frodo… If you don't mind, it's a Tuesday, and I'm on my way to buy some fucking milk! This is not Middle-Earth, this is the sidewalk, and that unicorn you're riding is my dog. So why don't you gather up all your hobbit friends and go back to the Shire."

While exiting the train we immediately set the following itinerary:

-Get high.

-Go to the Van Gogh Museum.

-Do mushrooms.

You may ask, "Why didn't you do mushrooms before going to the Van Gogh museum?" I'll tell you why. Because you would be stuck at the first painting for the better part of the afternoon, mouth agape, while families of tourists shoo their children around you, muttering under their breath, "He knows that's just the museum entrance sign, right?"

Before I continue I would just like to make a

public service announcement and say that I'm not recommending everyone do mushrooms. They're not for everyone. They're unpredictable and they come with a risk of losing your mind. I don't want anyone to approach me later burning with pent up hostility, "That wasn't cool man! I climbed a tree and cried for five hours."

There ended up only being 3 willing participants; my brother, our friend from the program Geraldo and me. Franklin was catching a train back to Italy and after considering it for a brief moment, used his better judgment not to do mushrooms on a fully-booked international train. Our friend Schneider had decided to sit this one out, as the previous night, awaiting our arrival, he had prematurely taken a batch. They didn't seem to work, so he went to bed in the communal hostel bedroom. About one hour after lights out, with a great surprise to both him and the German couple in the bunk bed adjacent to his, the high kicked in.

We went to a small shop that looked like a cross between a coffeehouse and a medieval apothecary. They presented us with a weathered leather-bound menu much like a wine list, but of mushroom varieties, full with name and description. Everything about this place reminded me of a wine tasting room, which amused me, because you can only take the whole wine analogy so far.

We open on a man in full golf garb at the
Country Club - surrounded by a group of
his sweater-vest wearing friends.
    "Me and the Mrs. are going to Napa this
    weekend. We have a pretty nice little
    vacation planned; eat at a five star
    restaurant, go to the spa, a couples
    mud bath… and then we are going to get
    out   of   our   skulls   high   on   wild
    mushrooms!"

I must admit, I would love to see someone participate in a mushroom tasting.

A sophisticated man elegantly leaning against a mahogany bar. He gently puts a mushroom cap in his mouth and swirls it around in his cheeks.
"A hint of manure… rainbows?" His eyes shift back and forth. "Oh, definitely rainbows!"
The man cleanses his palate with a toke from a joint resting in an ashtray beside him.
"I guess I'll try this one…" He slowly chews the new varietal. Suddenly he goes into a rage, spitting

and scraping his tongue. "Ahhh, Childhood fears! Inner demons, oh god!"

We eagerly huddled around the shared menu as we read and considered each mushroom one at a time.

The Psychedelic – On the light side, this mushroom offers great clarity and focus. Refreshing acidity, featuring vibrant structures and bright colors. The finish is more expressive with a leprechaun that rides on a magic carpet.

"Alright?"
Enticed we read on.

Fungi Disturbus – This fungi starts out with good intensity and turns a little crazy on the backend, featuring a long, dark finish that echoes in your mind like a scream in the night. BE EMOTIONALLY PREPARED.

"I don't even know what that last part means."

Eventually the group settled on a mushroom entitled "Philosopher Stones." Underneath it all, I think we chose this one because we had some crazy idea that it would be this wonderful sophisticated, existential experience. I had a premonition of us sitting in a circle; talking, exploring the laws of the universe, the meaning of life. But who were we kidding? You're eating mushrooms; you're probably going to spend the majority of the night staring at your hand in amazement.

"Look at my hand," said the typical mushroom-tripper with uncontrollable laughter as the tears filled his eyes. "I'm crying.... I'm crying rainbows!"

We threw the Philosopher Stones on a slice of pizza, choked them down and hit the streets waiting for them to kick in. Nothing. Then it hit us all at once, like when you're doing Jell-O shots, it's- candy, candy, candy, and... shitfaced.

I looked over at my brother and could see that they had hit him full bore as well. Now there is an important note to make here. When you are walking through Central Amsterdam there are these African immigrants who stroll the streets selling one of the few things that is illegal, cocaine. They sell cocaine to tourists, but they don't call it cocaine. Instead they very discretely, *in an obvious drug dealer type way*, walk alongside you, stop and deliver the code name by sharply whispering "Psst Charlie?" This happens to be my brother's name, Charlie.

So here he is wandering the streets of Holland, high-as-a-kite on a hallucinogenic while complete strangers briskly walk by whispering his name as if it were a question. "Pssst! Hey. Charlie? Charlie?" My brother shot me the same look I imagine the violinist gave the cellist as the Titanic went down. A look of both disbelief and subtle resignation, as if to say, "I guess this is really happening?" But of course I'm no help to him, because I'm no longer in the Netherlands. I'm in the netherworld, staring at my fingers while I laugh wildly "I'm crying rainbows!"

Ménage à Trois

When you are abroad for a decent length of time you have to get accustomed to short romances. How comfortable you can be in these brief flings really just comes down to how you feel about one-night stands. For me, it has always been a contentious subject. If when you say one-night stands you mean pick-up lines, fake laughs and beer goggles, if you mean awkward undressing, fleeting foreplay and unreciprocated sexual exertion, yea a night that comes with all of its disappointment, desperation, fornication and shame and shamelessness; leaving in its breech nothing but a sore heart, an itchy crotch and an unquenched craving, then certainly I am against them.

But if when you say one-night stands you mean fluttering anticipation, gravitational gaze, and electric lips, if you mean silver screen kisses, operatic moans, and encore performances, if you mean pure romance, if you mean the clandestine encounter that puts the spring in a young man's step on a frosty, crisp morning, if you mean newfound charisma, untamed pleasure and a wild story; which enables a man to magnify his joy, and his happiness, and to forget, if only for a little while, life's great tragedies, and heartaches, and sorrows, then certainly I am for them.

I awoke in an unfamiliar bed to the clattering of a window shutter and the dim melody of French coming through the bedroom's cracked door. The sheets were a lush red and the pillow smelled of a blissful aroma that immediately cascaded my memories, not of the night before, but of a girl I had a crush on one summer, and ran with in the park and kissed in the grass, and who left her scent on my shirt which I kept in my closet until the fragrance no longer cast its spell.

The night before was a faded alcohol infused fever dream and I could not grasp on to a single clue as to why I was in this apartment, in this bed, and who had been lying next to me in the space that was now empty, except for a wrinkled imprint.

We had been partying and dancing with a horde of internationals and I had been drinking Long Islands all night like it was...well...like it was iced tea.

I threw off the sheets, put on my pants and briefly scanned the room. There were two other beds in the room, one illuminated by the sun and the other off in the corner covered in pillows. I caught a glance of myself in the bedside mirror to discover hickeys and scratches on my neck and chest. *What kind of debauchery had happened the night before?* I had no idea. I found my torn shirt tossed in the middle of the room, obviously ripped off in the heat of passion.

In my pocket there's an unopened vending machine condom and my cell phone. I quickly look through the phone and see a suggestive text message from an unknown number reading:

Where are you? I am in bed now. The door is open.

Well that's great, it didn't really help me at all. I was there, she was no longer in bed and the window to the night before was foggy at best.

I assumed that I must be at the apartment of the three French girls in the program: Lucie, Celine and

Marguerite. Their country of origin was their only tying thread as they could not have been anymore dissimilar. You could imagine meeting them in entirely different environments: Lucie, maybe a chance happening at a makeshift bar at an exclusive art party in Paris, Celine perhaps under an umbrella on a vibrant beach in the Riviera and Marguerite at the supermarket; she's the semi-hot, kinda-cute checkout lady.

With no other leads, I decided that there was no other option than to continue my investigation in the next room. I shyly exited the bedroom to meet the three girls halfway through their breakfast. Coffee and brioches lay on the table along with the remnants of the party from the night before: empty wine bottles, stained glasses, half a bottle of Johnnie Walker and a single shot glass. I could only imagine that the whisky was my handy work and the culprit of my sustained amnesia. There was a blanket and a pillow on the tiny couch, which led me to believe that at least one of them slept in the living room.

"*Bonjour* Mike. Come have coffee."

"*Ciao belleze. Bonjour.*"

Lucie poured me a cup of pressed coffee and placed it in front of me on the table with the classic

French *voilà*. I had learned an important lesson the month before that it is essential to understand the subtle nuances of a language. I had been in Paris and heard *voilà* repeated quite frequently at restaurants and street food carts. The phrase means 'it is ready' or 'here it is,' but until that point I had only heard it used in a magic connotation, which made for some awkward exchanges the first two days in Paris; I thought all the food vendors were wannabe magicians. Each time I was presented a dish I consistently had the look of someone pointedly not impressed.

If you translated this look directly into words it would read something along the lines of "Oooh *voilà*, wow. Abracadabra, the croissant I just ordered. Amazing!" The whole time I was judging them and it turns out that I was the asshole American with a shitty attitude.

I slowly sipped my coffee and contemplated my next move as the girls made small talk. It was really quite an amazing lineup of suspects; the three girls all striking in their own way. Being that I didn't remember a damn thing from the night before, I found myself having the strangest feeling of being envious, of myself.

Lucie was like a mythical figure, the girl that everyone in the city desired and fanaticized about. A covergirl, a girl even the girls fell in love with. She carried herself with amazing confidence and was not only cool, but drop-dead gorgeous. She had cream skin, dark hair, forget-me-not blue eyes and ruby lips that curved in the way that models try to imitate and hold long enough for a camera flash.

Celine was standing by the sink smoking a cigarette. She was scantly clad in a long sleeping t-shirt that clung to her features and went down to her thin, tan legs, one of them perched on the other like that of an exotic flamingo. Somewhere beneath her playful bangs were eyes that were permanently squinted in such a way, almost like a cat; she always seemed as if she were either smiling, or stalking prey. You were never sure which it was.

And then there was Marguerite. It wasn't that she wasn't pretty, she was, but she always just looked so damned bored. She had the permanent disposition of a person that was losing a game of Monopoly.

When there was a brief pause in conversation I began my line of inquiry hoping that perhaps some ambiguous question or comment may lead to a break in the case. I scrambled through my mental facilities and was only able to come up with:

"Well, that was fun last night…"

I know, super brilliant. But for such a painfully un-strategic remark I gained a great amount of insight as Lucie smiled, Celine coyly raised her eyebrows and Marguerite rolled her eyes and scoffed like I just put a hotel on Park Place. I employed my powers of deduction and used the simple process of elimination to surmise that the pouty French scoffer was probably not the one that ripped my shirt off the night before.

Conversation continued as the girls talked of their recent trip to Rome and I fiddled with a wine cork. I felt like I was in a poker game waiting for someone to tip their hand so I could go all-in.

Lucie had an amazing magnetism when she spoke. If you believe eyes are the windows to the soul, then she was notorious for breaking and entering. When she spoke with you she would look right into you, like the conversation you were having was the most interesting interaction she had ever had and you were the only person worth a damn in the world.

Celine posed so sweetly in the corner in only her t-shirt. That t-shirt, she may as well have been naked. I tried my best not to drool and constantly shifted my eyes around the room in an attempt to seem like I wasn't tracing her small chest as it gently rose and fell with each breath.

When she got out a clear glass juicer and began squeezing an orange I lost my shit and knocked my coffee cup off the table.

"Ça va?" Lucie asked in mild concern.

I responded "Tres bién" in my French accent, which unfortunately is horribly forced and dangerously close to that of a certain cartoon skunk.

I really don't think women know how seductive they can be by just displaying their natural figure. I wish I had that same power, to be able to just devastate people with the slight hint of my undressed body. It is just something men cannot do. With women everything is just so luscious, smooth and curvy; while a naked man is just so…so…I think it is the flaccid penis. It's just not a good look. Every penis looks like it should have an accompanying adjective; like stumpy, clumsy or shrinky. If you ever go to a nude beach it feels like you are at a casting call for Snow White and the Seven Dwarfs; there's Sleepy, Dopey, Grumpy, Bashful, and you're just hoping Happy and Sneezy don't rear their ugly heads.

I queried further starting with direct questions, using the interrogation to slowly eliminate possibilities like a game of Battleship. I scored a direct hit when I asked Celine when she had woken up.

In a very French manner she responded:

"Too early, the sun always wakes me up."

And *voilà*, the mystery was solved. There was only one bed that was on the west wall and would get direct illuminating light from the morning sun, and with Marguerite already out of the running, there could only be one result – I had slept with Lucie. I had slayed the dragon. I wanted to yell declarations out the window. I wanted buy a train ticket to Rome just to run up the Spanish Steps to the Rocky theme song. I wanted to notch my belt, then frame it, and then mount it on the wall.

It is at this point that Marguerite, obviously tired with my game of 20 questions turns to me in a sarcastic almost snarky tone and says:

"And how are you feel today, Mike?"

I didn't hesitate.

"If you really want to know, I feel like a million bucks!"

Obviously this wasn't the right answer as Marguerite erupted in French curses.

Lucie told her to relax, but this only brought on a tirade. Continuing in French, Marguerite points at me and then the blanket on the couch. It's obvious that she's in some kind of jealous fit. I don't claim to speak French by any means, but I can catch a word here and there. She spoke of going to sleep, waking to my shirt being ripped, her trying her best to go back to sleep, but unable to due to the 'noises,' the 'animal noises,' which were too loud for her to bare, thus finally leaving the room to seek refuge on the uncomfortable couch.

It must have been too much for her, but who can really blame her? Sometimes when you shake the coconut tree the jungle sings, and who wants to sleep in a room while two other people are in the throws of ecstasy?

I just kind of shrugged, smiled and folded my hands behind my head, as I didn't really have anything to say. To be honest, I kind of wanted her to continue recounting the story. With no recollection myself I was extremely interested – *yeah animal noises? Tell me more about that.*

Celine was thoroughly amused by the whole situation and laughed all the way down the hall as she peeled off to take a shower.

I really didn't know what to say. I thought I might cut it with some pure honesty. Just out of earshot of

Lucie I whispered to Marguerite–

"Your roommate is hot. I don't know what you want me to say. I would do it all again in a heartbeat."

This sent her into a rage and she left the room in an uproar.

Lucie and I exchanged an uneasy smile.

"I'm sorry if I made things weird."

"Don't worry she will get over it. She likes you, she just didn't sleep well."

Now that I knew the *who*, I wanted to know the *how*. I had so many more questions. How did it start? How did it end? Was it as good for me as it was for you?

I decided to ask Lucie out for brunch when she dropped the big one.

"I wish I could, but… my boyfriend is on his way over."

Boyfriend? What is this boyfriend business? You have got to be kidding me.

"Boyfriend? Your boyfriend is coming here right now?"

She checked her watch and did some math in her head.

"Yeah, Marco should be here any minute."

"I should leave. I should go. I'm going to get out of here. Does he know I was here last night?"

"Oh don't worry he knows you were here last night. He is not the jealous type."

I already had two shoes on and one arm in the sleeve of my jacket. Fucking French with their open relationships and free love. What a weird culture. We just slept together last night - he's not jealous though – oh, okay, let's all sit around a table and talk as my hickeys hang out of my shirt and your volatile roommate slams doors.

My moral compass was set nowhere near to True North, but this was too much. I bailed down the stairs of the apartment building to avoid a possible awkward elevator confrontation and went out the side of the apartment complex.

Once I was on the street, I lit a cigarette and was about to reflect upon my adventure and conquest when I saw a fluttering piece of fabric on the metal gate that separated the apartment's courtyard and the street.

This literal shred of evidence unraveled all my fantasies, the tectonic plates shifted underneath my feet and all of the puzzle pieces fell directly into place. The clue illuminated a whole other chain of events that filled itself in bit by bit.

The fabric was unmistakable, partly because I was wearing the rest of it as a shirt. The shirt hadn't been ripped off by a lust-filled vixen at all, but had been torn when a drunk, horny American who had locked himself out of an apartment building on his way out to buy condoms from a vending machine, scaled a metal fence that also, guess what, scraped and bruised his chest and neck. With beer goggles strapped tight on my head I must have been trying my best to grab the low hanging fruit, laying it on pretty hard in the ten-items or less line. While I was out I must have gotten hastily lost and received a pretty straightforward text reading:

Where are you? I am in bed now. The door is open.

When I made it back to the apartment in my drunken stupor I passed out in Marguerite's bed and snored like an animal, until she could not handle it anymore and moved to a sitting couch in the living room in an effort to get some sleep, only to be mocked the next morning by a guy that not only didn't apologize, but told everyone how well rested he felt in U.S. dollars.

I then sat there hands folded behind my head with an idiotic *Cool Hand Luke* smile on my face conjuring up some creepy first person, half-baked dramatization of a classic folktale where Goldilocks returns to the scene of the crime and I try to figure out whose porridge I stuck my ladle in. To add insult to injury I proceeded to tell the poor girl I had been relentlessly pursuing the night before that her roommate was hotter than she was and I would do it again, 'in a heartbeat' I might add. Then I scampered out of the apartment in some half crazed stumble and stutter. It wasn't my finest moment.

On my way home I tried to daydream, if just for a little while; of what the one-night stand would have been like, with all of its desperation, fornication and shame and shamelessness, yea a night complete with its awkward undressing, fleeting foreplay and unreciprocated sexual exertion.

MIKE LEMCKE

ACKNOWLEDGMENTS

I would like to express my gratitude to the many people who saw me through the writing of this book; to all those who have provided support, to my wonderfully creative friends who listened to rough drafts at talent night parties, to Northern Californian crowds that helped me edit early versions through laughter, and to those that listened to the stories when forced into casual conversations.

I would like to thank my brother who helped me form my sense of humor and pursue my dreams. You have always been there for me, even like that one time when I couldn't find my car.

I would like to thank Ryan Hedrick for his generous help reading endless drafts, talking things over and offering comments to make the stories the best they could be.

Thanks to Patricia Willers who helped correct some of my horrible grammar and encouraged me to publish this work.

Above all, I would like to thank my amazing wife Maja for her loving encouragement.

MIKE LEMCKE

ABOUT THE AUTHOR

Mike Lemcke wants to live in a world where people can laugh at funerals, drink at museums and check out of hotels at 2 p.m. As a comedian, he has been applauded for his stand-up performances, honored for his short film directing and widely panned for his acting abilities. When he is not scribbling into a notebook or standing in the back of a comedy club feeling envious of a well-written joke, he can be found drinking at a barbeque in Northern California or a coffee shop in Stockholm.

www.ingramcontent.com/pod-product-compliance
Lightning Source LLC
Chambersburg PA
CBHW030555130626
46552CB00006B/2558